To Liam and Anouska, with love
— C. F.

For Lorcan, Mark and Gerry, and, as ever, Tiziana
— J. B-B.

First published in Great Britain in 2002 by Little Tiger Press, London.

Library of Congress Cataloging-in-Publication Data available
ISBN 0-439-47106-0

10 9 8 7 6 5 4 3 2 1 03 04 05 06 07

Printed in Belgium
First Scholastic edition, June 2003

Hushabye Lily

By Claire Freedman
Illustrated by John Bendall-Brunello

ORCHARD BOOKS • NEW YORK
AN IMPRINT OF SCHOLASTIC INC.

Nighttime crept over the farmyard. The moon rose higher into the darkening sky.

"Are you still awake, Lily?" asked Mother Rabbit. "You should be fast asleep by now."

"I'm trying, but I can't sleep," Lily replied. "The farmyard's much too noisy for sleeping."

She pricked up her ears.

"What's that quacking sound I hear?" she asked.

“Hush now,” said Mother Rabbit. “It’s only the ducks resting in the tall reeds.”

“Sorry, Lily!” one of the ducks called out.

"Are we keeping you awake? We were only singing sleepy bedtime songs to one another. Would you like me to sing a song to you, too?"

"Yes, please!" said Lily.

QUAAACK

So the duck puffed out his chest, shook out his feathers, and sang the most beautiful duck lullaby he knew.

"That was lovely!" said Lily, sighing sleepily.

"Shhh," whispered the duck. And without a sound, he waddled away, back to the moonlit pond.

“Whoo, whoo!”
hooted the owl
on the barn roof.

“Hush!” whispered
Lily’s mother.

The owl flew away,
high into the sky.

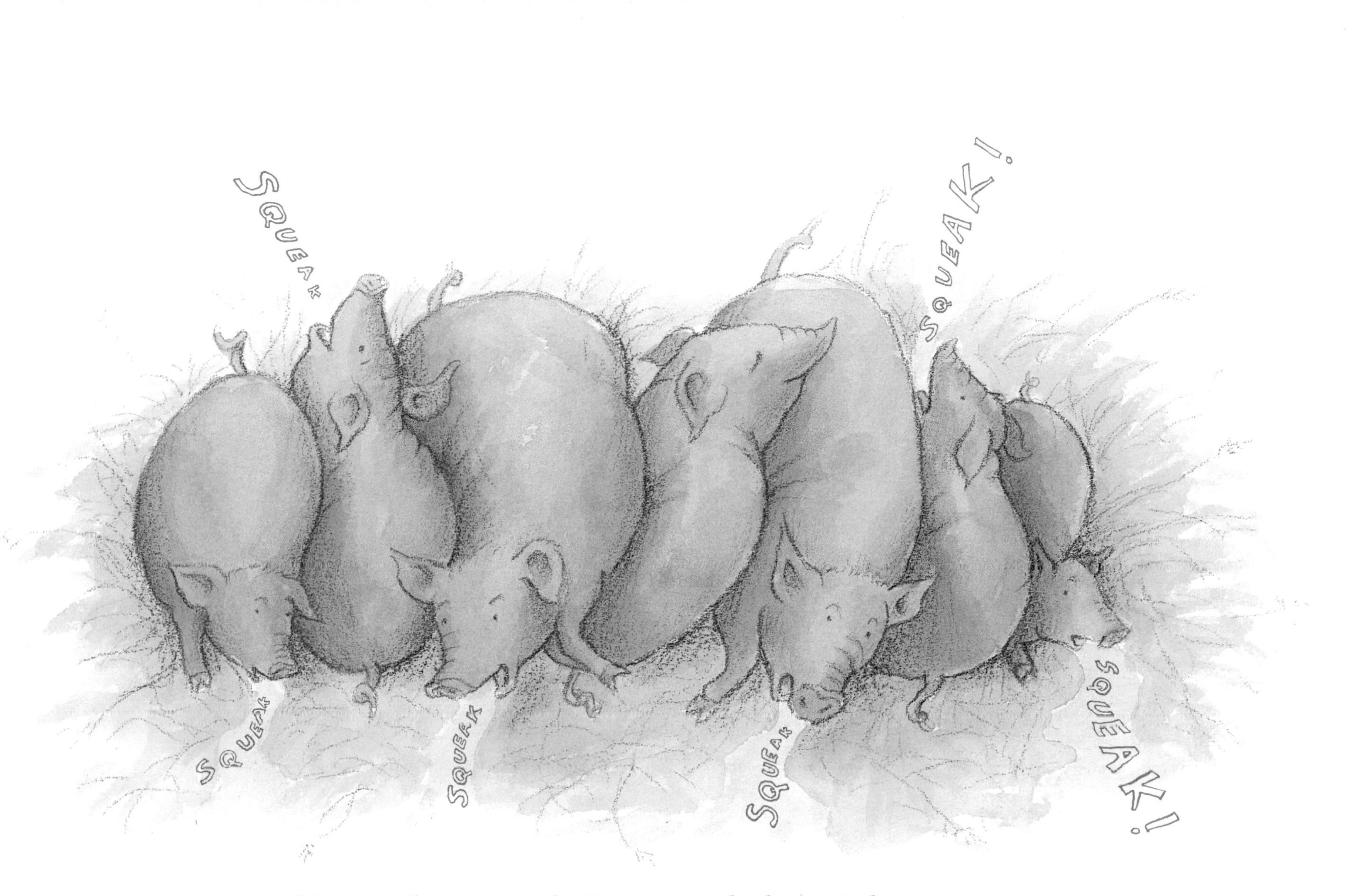

"Squeak, squeak," yawned the piglets, nestling top-to-tail in the pigsty.

"Shhh," said Mother Rabbit. "Hush!"

Sleepily, Lily closed her eyes . . .

. . . but before long she opened them again and pricked up her ears.

"What's that mooing I hear?" she asked.

"Hush now!" said Mother Rabbit. "It's only the cows mooing in the barn."

"Sorry, Lily!" cried out a soft-eyed cow.

"Are we keeping you awake? We were only telling each other bedtime stories. Would you like to hear a story, too?"

"Ooh, yes, please!" said Lily.

So the cow told Lily her favorite sleepy bedtime tale.

"That was nice!" said Lily with a huge yawn.

"Shhh," whispered the cow. And she lumbered back to the old barn as quietly as she could.

"Meow!" cried the farm cat,
huddling her kittens together.

MEOW

"Hee-haw!" brayed the dreaming donkey, turning in his sleep.

"Shhh," said Lily's mother. "Hush now!" Lily closed her eyes . . .

. . . but then she opened them again and pricked up her ears.

"What's that clucking sound I hear?" she asked.

"Hush," said Mother Rabbit. "It's only the hens hiding in the haystacks."

"Sorry, Lily!" called out a bright-eyed hen.

"Are we keeping you awake? We were only collecting straw to make our beds more comfortable. Shall I find some straw for you, too?"

"I'd like that," said Lily.

So the hen brought back a beakful of straw and tucked it under Lily's head.

"That's cozy," said Lily, struggling to keep her eyes open.

"Shhh," whispered the hen, and she crept softly on tiptoes to the henhouse.

"Shhh," hushed the ducks
to the rippling reeds.

"Shhh," hushed the cows
to the leaves on the trees.

"Shhh," hushed the hens
into the whispering wind.

"Hush now, Lily," whispered Mother Rabbit,
and she snuggled up to her little one.

The moon hid behind the clouds.
All was quiet and still until . . .

. . . down in the shadowy stable, a little brown foal opened his eyes and pricked up his ears.

"What's that whistling sound I hear?" he asked.

"Shhh, go back to sleep," his mother whispered. "It's only little Lily snoring!"